I Celebrate
Nature

◆ —— DEDICATION —— ◆

TO THE CREATOR—
and to Michele, Kristin, Robert, Vanessa and Tyler

with special thanks to
Katie Agbulos
Steve Nghyen
Amanda Glenn

ISBN paperback 1-883220-00-9
ISBN hardback 1-883220-01-7

Published by Dawn Publications
14618 Tyler Foote Road
Nevada City, CA 95959
800-545-7475

Printed on recycled paper
using soy based ink

10 9 8 7 6 5 4 3 2 1
First Edition

Designed by LeeAnn Brook
Type Style is Berkeley

I Celebrate Nature

Written and Illustrated by
Diane Iverson

A NOTE TO PARENTS AND TEACHERS

Children are born with a sense of curiosity, joy and wonder about the natural world. They delight in picking weed bouquets, climbing trees and stomping their feet in mud puddles. As adults, we can encourage and share in this experience of oneness with nature. The more children feel their connection with the rest of creation, the more they will want to live in harmony with God's other creatures, rather than cause them harm.

In creating **I Celebrate Nature** my goal is to help you encourage a sense of discovery in your little ones, and perhaps even nourish the healthy child inside of you. While the pictures are realistic as far as attention to detail, I have taken the liberty of showing the children in a variety of seasons and settings and have not drawn in their adult chaperones.

I feel that if we teach a conservation ethic through the books and magazines we select for our families, as well as through personal example, our children will be better prepared to preserve that which past generations have gone so far toward destroying. That is the dream behind this book.

Diane Iverson

I celebrate nature

with its green and golden trees.

I walk softly among the butterflies

and creatures running free.

I love to chatter with the birds

and watch them fly up in the air.

I help the puffballs scatter seeds

through meadows broad and fair.

I feel the skipping, dancing water

and the crunch of autumn leaves.

I hear the far coyote
and the gentle buzz of bees.

I'm grateful for these creatures

and the world that we share,

and try to find some little way

to show them that I care.

ABOUT THE AUTHOR

Diane Iverson is a wildlife artist with a special interest in the birds and mammals of North America.  She enjoys camping and backpacking with her husband, Doug, and devotes a great deal of time to conservation education programs in the public school system. Diane has a strong conservation ethic, a love for children and a deep fascination with children's books. She is also the illustrator of **Buttons the Foster Bunny**.

ACKNOWLEDGEMENTS

I am blessed by the generous support of the following people who helped with the creation of this book: my husband Doug, who is my photographer, backpacking partner, and constant source of encouragement; my publisher Bob, who has made the whole process run smoothly and pleasantly; Michael, for his editorial expertise and enthusiasm; LeeAnn, for all her contributions in the important area of design; and to the rest of the staff at Dawn Publications. Thanks also to the many teachers and school librarians who continually give me their valuable feedback.